# How Santa Got His Job

## By **Stephen Krensky**

## Illustrated by **S. D. Schindler**

**Aladdin Paperbacks**

New York  London  Toronto  Sydney  Singapore

First Aladdin Paperbacks edition October 2002
Text copyright © 1998 by Stephen Krensky
Illustrations copyright © 1998 by S. D. Schindler

ALADDIN PAPERBACKS
An imprint of Simon & Schuster
Children's Publishing Division
1230 Avenue of the Americas
New York, NY 10020

Also available in a Simon & Schuster Books for Young Readers hardcover edition.
Designed by Paul Zakris
The text of this book was set in 16-point Daily News Medium.
Drawings were done in ink using brush or rapidograph.
Printed in Hong Kong
2 4 6 8 10 9 7 5 3 1

The Library of Congress has cataloged the hardcover edition as follows:
Krensky, Stephen
How Santa got his Job / Stephen Krensky ; illustrated by S.D. Schindler.
p. cm.
Summary: Santa tries his hand at many jobs before finding the perfect job as the world's greatest gift giver.
ISBN 0-689-80697-3 (hc)
1. Santa Claus—Juvenile fiction. [1. Santa Claus—Fiction. 2. Occupations—Fiction. 3. Humorous stories.]
I. Schindler, S. D., ill. II. Title.
PZ7.K883Ho 1998
[E]—dc21
97-23474

ISBN 0-689-84668-1 (Aladdin pbk.)

For my mother-in-law, Mary Frongello,
who has worked closely with Santa for many years
—S. K.

To Paige, Lisa, Janet, Bernadette, and Keri
for keeping us elves working . . .
—S. D. S.

**W**hen Santa Claus was a young man,
he went out looking for a job.
Santa wanted no part of desks or offices.
He liked to stay on the move.

His first job was cleaning chimneys.
Santa was sure-footed on even the steepest roofs,
and he loved twisting through the tight spaces.

But there was a problem.

Santa was so neat that he never got covered in soot
or made a mess in the fireplace.

So nobody believed him when he said he was done.

"Where's the proof?" said some.

"You're not even dirty!" said others.

This led to a lot of arguments.

Santa worked for the post office next—
where everyone could see that he was doing his job.
Santa's favorite part was bringing packages to people all over town.
Waiting in traffic was frustrating, though.
"It's silly to waste all this time," he decided.
To speed things up, he started making deliveries in the middle of the night.

But there was a problem.
No one was glad to see him at that hour.
The postmaster got so many complaining letters
that Santa had to leave.

Since Santa had discovered he enjoyed staying up late,
he tried cooking at an all-night diner.
It felt good to fill orders for customers.
Sometimes Santa even surprised people with extra helpings.
"Oh, I couldn't eat another bite," many of them insisted.
"Well, maybe just one."

But there was a problem.
Every night Santa tasted and sampled and tasted some more
before he brought anything out of the kitchen.
He gained a lot of weight.

Hoping to get some exercise,
Santa then found a spot at the zoo.
He was very organized about the animals.
"I know when they are sleeping," said Santa,
"and when they are awake."
Over time he also learned
whether they were behaving themselves—or not.

But there was a problem.
Santa became close friends with the reindeer
and all the other animals got jealous.
Sadly, the zookeeper had to let him go.

By now, Santa was starting to get discouraged.
He didn't even notice what the reindeer were doing behind him.

They worked hard to cheer him up.

Together, they joined the circus.
Soon the reindeer were shooting Santa out of a cannon
three times a night.
Santa liked flying through the air
and wearing his new costume.
He was a big success.

But there was a problem.

The ringmaster wanted to build up the suspense.

"You need to look frightened," he told Santa.

"We want the crowd to worry about you."

But Santa was having too much fun for that.

"Ho, ho, ho!" he always cried

as he flew through the air.

So the crowd wasn't worried at all.

The angry ringmaster soon fired Santa and the reindeer.
As they gathered their things,
some elves came looking for autographs.
When they heard the news,
they invited Santa and the reindeer home for supper.

The elves lived way out of town.
They were toymakers, and their house was their workshop.

Santa was amazed.

"Children must love these toys," he said.

The elves looked embarrassed.

They only made toys for their own pleasure.

Selling them was too much trouble.

"What if you give them away?" Santa asked.

The elves hadn't thought of that.

"I could deliver them for you," Santa offered.

There were enough toys here for children all over the world.

The elves smiled—and hired him on the spot.

The elves made Santa a special sack
that was always big enough
no matter how many toys were put in it.
Then they built him a sleigh.

The polar bears offered to pull it.
They were very strong—and whipped Santa across the snow.
But there was a problem.

It was the biggest one yet.

To Santa's surprise, this problem could be solved.

Santa and the reindeer practiced together every day.
They made a few mistakes at first,
but soon they learned to work as a team.

In the darkest part of winter,
when people need their spirits lifted the most,
Santa got ready to go.

As the elves said good-bye, they gave Santa an emergency kit.
It held a compass, ski goggles, cough drops,
and other things.
Santa thanked them very much.
All his jobs had taught him it was good to be prepared.

Then Santa and his reindeer took off.
That first night was a little hard,
because Santa was still learning about shortcuts and high winds.
But at last he got the hang of it.

Ever since then, the elves have made toys all year
—and Santa has given them away in one night.
He loves his job as much as ever,
and he's gotten pretty good at it over the years.
Still, he always keeps his emergency kit close by

because no job is perfect.